Molly Bannaky

D1445725

For my husband, Marion McGill,
and my daughters, Gwendolyn and Paulette
—A. M.

I dedicate this book to all the teachers in the world
for their tireless and compassionate efforts to educate our future.
Thank you.
—C. K. S.

The text was set in 14-point Minion Semibold.
The illustrations are watercolor on illustration board.

Library of Congress Cataloging-in-Publication Data

McGill, Alice.
Molly Bannaky / by Alice McGill; illustrated by Chris Soentpiet.
p. cm.
Summary: Relates how Benjamin Banneker's grandmother journeyed from England to Maryland in the late
seventeenth century, worked as an indentured servant, began a farm of her own, and married a freed slave.
HC ISBN-13: 978-0-395-72287-9   PA ISBN-13: 978-0-547-07676-8
1. Banneker, Benjamin, 1731–1806 — Family — Juvenile fiction.
[1. Banneker, Benjamin, 1731–1806 — Family — Fiction. 2. Farm life — Fiction.] I. Soentpiet, Chris, ill. II. Title.
PZ7.M478468Ban 1999
[E]'—dc20   96-3000 CIP AC

Printed in Singapore.
TWP 10 9 8

Molly Bannaky

written by Alice McGill   *pictures by* Chris K. Soentpiet

HOUGHTON MIFFLIN HARCOURT
BOSTON · NEW YORK

On a cold, gray morning in 1683, Molly Walsh sat on a stool, tugging at the udder of an obstinate cow. She was a dairymaid, and it was her duty to get up every morning around five o'clock and go to that same shed and milk that same cow. The man who owned the cow owned the cottage where she lived, the manor house, and all the land around. He was lord.

Molly kept tugging. The milk squirted into the pail. When the pail was full, it was her duty to take it up the hill to the manor house and hand it to the scullery maid, who handed it to the kitchen maid, who handed it to the cook. The jittery cow kept hooking its head. The week before, the cow had kicked over her pail of milk. The cook had warned Molly that she would be brought before the court if ever again she stole his lordship's milk. That was the law.

Molly's shawl was thin; her hands were very cold. But at last the pail was full to the frothy brim. Suddenly Molly sneezed. The cow jumped, the pail tipped over, and the milk seeped into the damp ground. Before the sun set that day, Molly stood before the court. The usual penalty was death on the gallows, but no one who could read the Bible could be executed for stealing. So a Bible was offered to her. That, too, was the law. Molly's voice rang out clear and true.

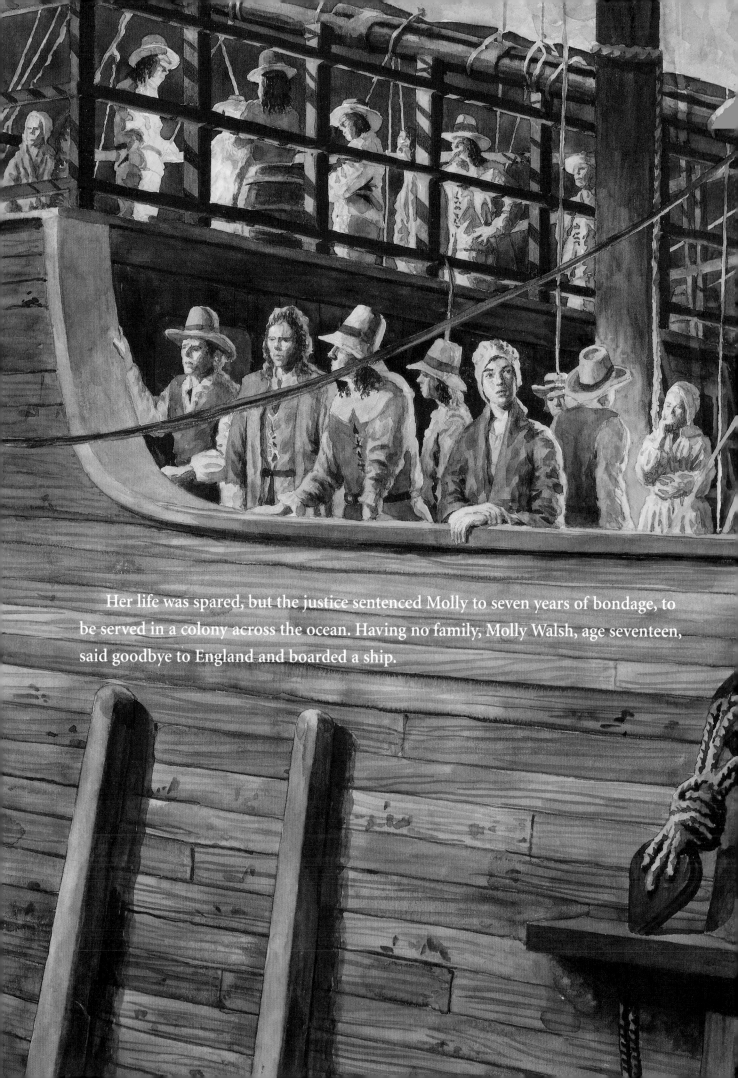

Her life was spared, but the justice sentenced Molly to seven years of bondage, to be served in a colony across the ocean. Having no family, Molly Walsh, age seventeen, said goodbye to England and boarded a ship.

After she landed in the New World, Molly worked for a planter on the eastern shore of Maryland. There the cannons fired at daybreak, calling the servants to work. Molly tended her master's tobacco crops, pressing the tiny brown seeds into the earth and picking the worms from the flowering stalks. Her callused hands grew strong enough to control a team of oxen and to hold the plow steady. In her spare time, Molly sewed and nursed the sick for pay.

After working for the planter for seven years, Molly was free to go. As the law required, the farmer gave her an ox hitched to a cart, a plow, two hoes, a bag of tobacco seeds, a bag of seed corn, clothing, and a gun. Acres and acres of fertile land stretched ahead of her. Just before sunset that same day, Molly left the road and went four miles into the wilderness, where she staked her claim.

That a lone woman should stake land was unheard of, but Molly's new neighbors saw the way she jutted out her chin. They helped her build a one-room cabin. They helped her harvest and cure her first crop. They helped her cart the tobacco to the warehouse to sell. But Molly soon realized that the farm was too much for her to manage alone.

One day Molly read a posted announcement that a ship would be landing soon.
Because she needed help in working her land, she decided to watch the docking of
this ship—a slave ship. She watched the men of Africa file by, one after the other.
She saw the misery, anger, and shame on their faces as they were forced to mount the
auction block. Then Molly noticed a tall, regal man who dared to look into the eyes
of every bidder. Molly bought him and vowed to treat him well and set him free just
as soon as her land was cleared.

Molly talked to this man, using her hands and arms to tell him of her homeland and of her years as an indentured servant. He smiled at this strange-looking woman, with sweet-grass eyes and straw hair and skin the color of the underside of a melon. He told her his name: Bannaky.

Because he was not used to the climate, he was often sick with chills and fever. Still, Bannaky would walk up and down the rows of tobacco, stopping to turn each leaf on a stalk as if reading a printed page. He showed Molly how to dig ditches to guide streams of water down the furrows.

As the tobacco ripened in the fields, Molly and Bannaky grew to love each other. She signed his freedom papers, and a traveling minister performed their marriage rites. Though Molly had broken colonial law by marrying a black man, her neighbors came to accept this marriage and to respect Bannaky. In times of drought he shared his knowledge of irrigation and crop rotation, learned at an early age in his native country.

Years passed. Molly and Bannaky had four young daughters. A large house and many outbuildings overlooked their hundred acres of land.